The Three Little Gators

Helen
Ketteman

Illustrated by
Will Terry

www.av2books.com

Your AV² Media Enhanced book gives you a fiction readalong online.
Log on to www.av2books.com and enter the unique book code from
this page to use your readalong.

AV² Readalong Navigation

Go to **www.av2books.com**,
and enter this book's
unique code.

BOOK CODE

L 5 0 0 6 7 8

AV² by Weigl brings you media
enhanced books that support
active learning.

First Published by

**ALBERT
WHITMAN
& COMPANY**

Publishing children's books since 1919

**HIGHLIGHTED
TEXT**

**START
READING**

READ

PAGE TURNING

BACK NEXT

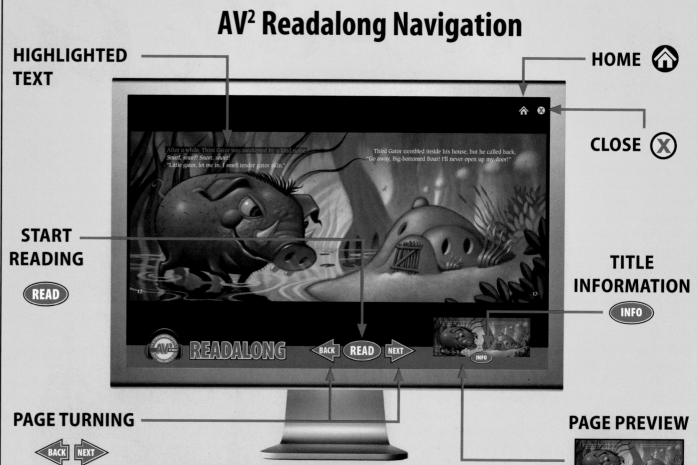

HOME

CLOSE

**TITLE
INFORMATION**

INFO

PAGE PREVIEW

Published by AV² by Weigl
350 5ᵗʰ Avenue, 59ᵗʰ Floor New York, NY 10118
Copyright ©2013 AV² by Weigl
All rights reserved. No part of this publication may be reproduced, stored in a retrieval system, or transmitted in any form or by any
means, electronic, mechanical, photocopying, recording, or otherwise, without the prior written permission of the publisher.

Printed in the United States of America in North Mankato, Minnesota
1 2 3 4 5 6 7 8 9 0 16 15 14 13 12

Text copyright © 2009 by Helen Ketteman.
Illustrations copyright © 2009 by Will Terry.
Published in 2009 by Albert Whitman & Company.

052012
WEP160512

Library of Congress Cataloging-in-Publication Data
Ketteman, Helen.
 The three little gators / Helen Ketteman ; illustrated by Will Terry.
   p. cm.
 Summary: In this adaptation of the traditional folktale, three little gators each build their house in an east Texas swamp, hoping for protection from the Big-bottomed
Boar.
 ISBN 978-1-61913-140-8 (hardcover : alk. paper)
 [1. Folklore.] I. Terry, Will, 1966- ill. II. Three little pigs. English. III. Title.
 PZ8.1.K54Th 2012
 398.2--dc23
 [E]   2012021692

2

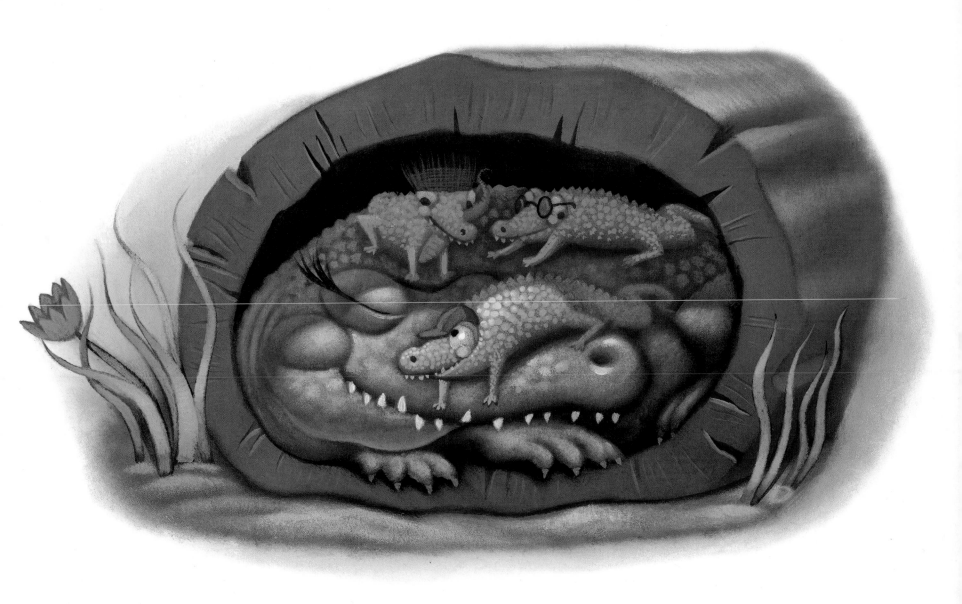

Once, three little gators lived with
their mama in an east Texas swamp.

One day, Mama said, "It's time you young 'uns set out on your own. Make sure you build houses strong enough to keep you safe from Big-bottomed Boar. Tasty, tender gators are his favorite snack."

4

So the three little gators set off.

Soon, they came upon some rocks. "Aha!" said First Gator.
"A house of rocks would be safe from Big-bottomed Boar."
"Bad choice," said Second Gator. "Rocks are heavy and too
much work."

6

"*Way* too much work," said Third Gator.
"Heavy or not, I'll build my house with rocks." First Gator began rolling rocks into a pile. His brothers waved good-bye and walked on, until . . .

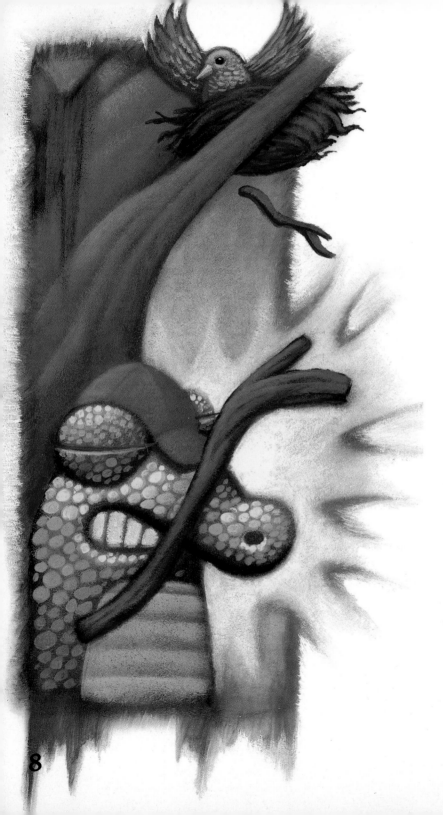

Plonk! A stick landed on Second Gator's head.

He looked up. In the tree above him, Hawk was building a nest. "Aha! I'll build a stick house. That will be easier."

"Bad choice," said Third Gator. "It's still too much work."

Third Gator waved good-bye and walked on, until . . .

Sloosh! Third Gator came to a river. He stopped to rest on the soft, damp sand along the riverbank. "Aha! A house of sand would be the easiest one to build," he said.

He pushed the sand into a big pile and dug a tunnel. Then he made a door from branches.

"Ha!" Third Gator laughed. "Big-bottomed Boar won't even know this is a house." And with that, he crawled in and fell asleep.

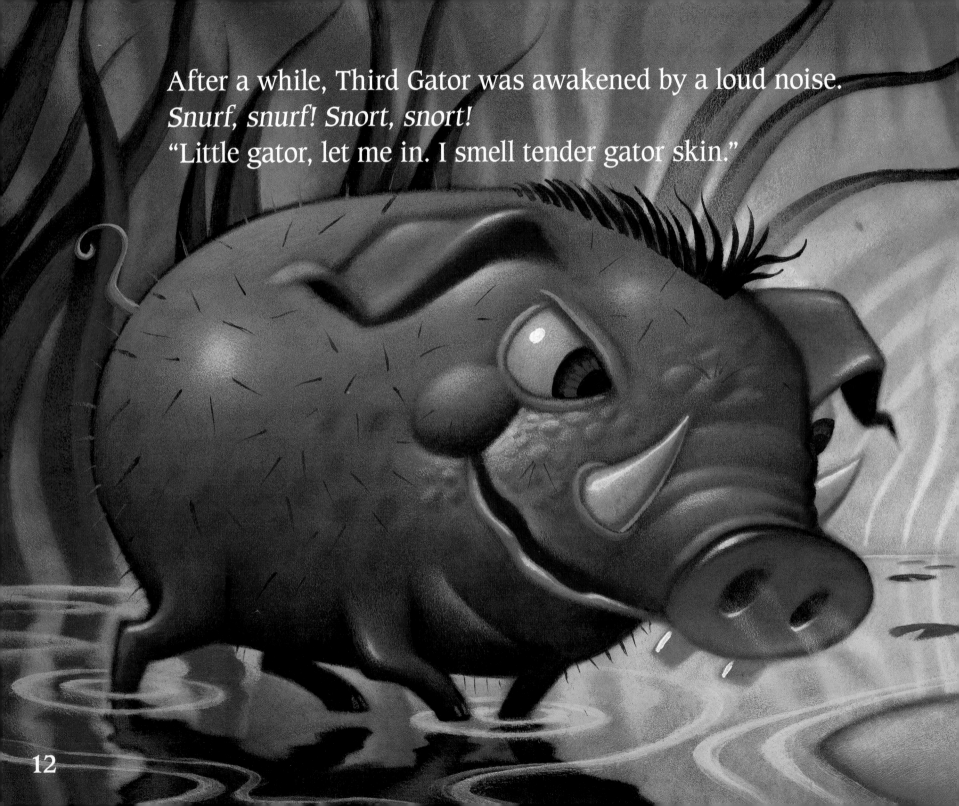

After a while, Third Gator was awakened by a loud noise.
Snurf, snurf! Snort, snort!
"Little gator, let me in. I smell tender gator skin."

12

Third Gator trembled inside his house, but he called back,
"Go away, Big-bottomed Boar! I'll never open up my door!"

"Then I'll wiggle my rump with a bump, bump, bump and smash your house!" Big-bottomed Boar wiggled his bottom and bumped it against Third Gator's house.

14

Sand flew everywhere.

Third Gator ran faster than a fox after a muskrat.
He scrambled through the brambles to Second Gator's house.

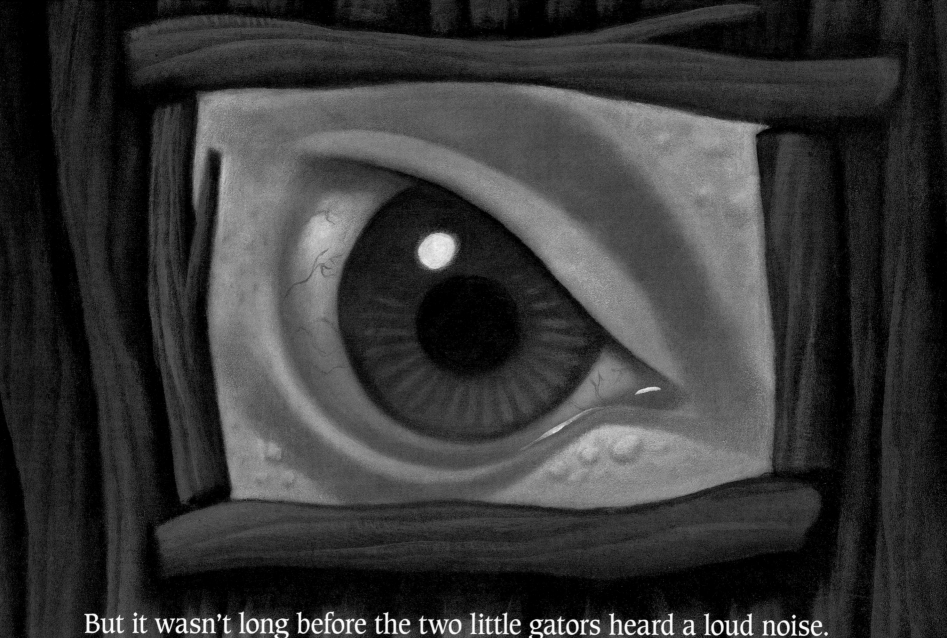

But it wasn't long before the two little gators heard a loud noise.
Snurf, snurf! Snort, snort!
"Little gators, let me in. I smell *two* tender gator skins.
Chasing you has made me thinner. I need two little gators for my dinner!"

The two little gators shivered at the sound of
Big-bottomed Boar's raspy voice, but they answered,
"Go away, Big-bottomed Boar! We'll never open up
the door!"

"Then I'll wiggle my rump with a **bump, bump, bump** and smash your house!" answered Big-bottomed Boar.

He wiggled his bottom and
bumpity-bumped it
against Second Gator's house.
Sticks flew everywhere.

21

Second Gator and Third Gator raced faster than snakes after a bullfrog. They rushed through the brush to First Gator's house.

But it wasn't long before the three little gators heard a loud noise.
Snurf, snurf! Snort, snort!
"Little gators, let me in.
I smell *three* tender gator skins.
Chasing you has made me thinner.
I need **three** little gators for
my dinner."

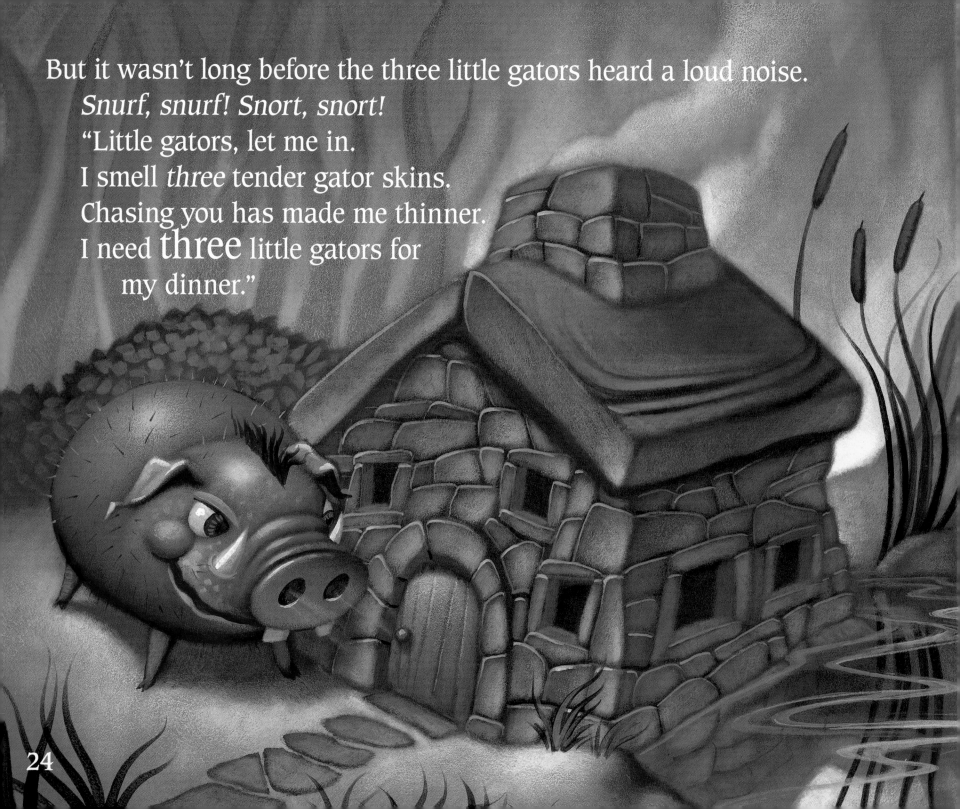

The three little gators shook at the sound of Big-bottomed Boar's terrible voice, but they called back, "We'll never open up the door! Go away, Big-bottomed Boar!"

"Then I'll wiggle my rump with a **bump, bump, bump** and smash your house!" answered Big-bottomed Boar. He wiggled and bumped, and waggled and thumped, but he could not smash First Gator's house.

26

"I'll get you yet!" Big-bottomed Boar snorted.

He climbed on the roof and squeezed into the chimney.

He grunted and wheezed and snorted and sneezed
as he inched his way down.

But the three little gators were ready for him. "Bad choice!" they called.

When Big-bottomed Boar finally dropped out of the chimney, he landed right on the hot grate of First Gator's barbecue grill.

Boar Sauce

30

Grill stripes burned into his big bottom, and
Big-bottomed Boar raced out of the house faster
than a thunderbolt!

Then Second Gator and Third Gator went outside and began piling up rocks.

"Good choice!" said First Gator, and he helped them build strong houses.

And Big-bottomed Boar never bumped his big, striped rump their way again.